Wicked Catch!

Rob Childs

Illustrated by Michael Reid

WICKED CATCH!

A CORGI PUPS BOOK : 9780552547925

First published in Great Britain by Corgi Books
an imprint of Random House Children's Books

This edition published 2003

7 9 10 8 6

The Random House Group Limited supports The Forest Stewardship
Council (FSC), the leading international forest certification organisation.
All our titles that are printed on Greenpeace approved FSC certified paper
carry the FSC logo. Our paper procurement policy can be found at:
www.rbooks.co.uk/environment.

Set in 18/25pt Bembo MT Schoolbook by
Falcon Oast Graphic Art Ltd.

Corgi Pups Books are published by Random House Children's Books,
61–63 Uxbridge Road, London W5 5SA,
A Random House Group Company

Addresses for companies within The Random House Group Limited
can be found at: www.randomhouse.co.uk/offices.htm

THE RANDOM HOUSE GROUP Limited Reg. No. 954009

A CIP catalogue record for this book
is available from the British Library.

Made and printed in Great Britain by
Cox & Wyman Ltd, Reading, Berkshire.

www.kidsatrandomhouse.co.uk

Contents

Series Reading Consultant: Prue Goodwin,
National Centre for Language and Literacy,
University of Reading

Chapter One
Fun and Games

"No-ball!" cried the batter. "Rubbish!" exclaimed the bowler. "You could've hit that."

"Oh, yeah?" Jagdish sneered, stretching out with his rounders bat to show how wide the ball had gone. "I'd have needed a fence post to reach it."

 "You *can* move your feet, you know," Lee told him. "You're not nailed to the ground."

"About time you learned to bowl straight."

Lee chuckled. "That makes the ball too easy to hit. I want to keep the batters guessing."

"Huh! What you mean is, stupid, *you've* got no idea where the ball's going either. It's all over the place."

"That's the spin I put on it."

"Spin!" Jagdish scoffed. "I'll tell you where your next ball's going – right over the hedge into them gardens."

Lee grinned and prepared to bowl again. He skipped across the bowling square, swinging his right arm back and forwards, then twisted his fingers as he released the ball.

Jagdish kept his eyes fixed
firmly on the swirling ball and
made good solid contact with
the bat.

Clunk!

To his delight, the ball soared
high into the sky. . .

. . .but what goes up must come down.

To his dismay, as he set off round the track, Jagdish realized that the ball hadn't flown quite as far as he'd boasted.

"Catch it!"
Lee's scream made
one of the fielders
stop what she was
doing – practising
handstands for
the gym club
after school.

Shannon had been placed near the hedge because of her long throws, but this was the first time that the ball had come her way. She didn't even have to move.

She simply reached up and plucked the ball out of the air as easily as picking an apple off a tree.

"Wicked!" whooped Lee. "Great catch, Shazza!"

Jagdish threw the bat away in disgust and it skidded across the grass towards the school building.

Fortunately for him, his tantrum wasn't seen by their teacher. Mrs Davison was working on fielding skills with the other half of her class.

Unfortunately, it *was* spotted by the caretaker. The bat finished up very close to where Mr Smith was stirring a pot of red paint, waiting for the Year 4 Games session to end so that he could get on with his own work in peace.

"Oi! You little horror!" he yelled. "I've a good mind to report you."

Jagdish ignored the threat and slumped to the ground, leaving the bat where it lay.

The caretaker went on grumbling to himself. "Roll on half-term!" he muttered. "That's what I say. . ."

Chapter Two
See Red

"Oi! Get away from that door. I've just painted it," shouted Mr Smith across the play-ground. "Clear off home."

Jagdish pulled a face at the caretaker and then bent down to tie a loose shoelace.

He was still feeling in a bad mood after Games.

"Roll-On should've put a warning sign up," said Lee. "Y'know, saying 'Wet Paint'."

"Bet he can't even spell it," Jagdish sneered. "He'd probably have written 'Wet Pants'!"

"You could do with a notice like that."

Jagdish twisted round and cursed. There was a patch of red paint on the seat of his trousers.

He stormed inside to change back into his shorts. "Right, Roll-On," he growled under his breath. "I'm gonna get even with you for this."

There was no one else around
when Jagdish re-emerged and
he saw his chance for swift
revenge. There was a tray of
paint lying in the playground
and he dipped his left hand
into it.

Jagdish sneaked towards the
caretaker's cottage nearby and
saw that its bright red front door
was also freshly painted.

"Huh! Bet old Roll-On's not
had to buy his own paint for that
job," he muttered. "Well he can
have some more of it for free..."

Jagdish pressed his sticky hand against the garden fence twice, leaving large smudged prints on the white panels. He didn't even hear the caretaker creep up behind him.

"You little hooligan!" yelled Mr Smith. "Caught you red-handed!"

Jagdish had to spend the next
two lunchtimes painting the
whole fence red.

His older brother, Suresh, couldn't resist coming to taunt him. "Nice to see you doing some work for a change, little brother."

Jagdish turned and scowled. "Push off!" he hissed. "I want to get this finished before the bell goes."

Suresh dribbled his football
along a path up to the fence to
inspect it more closely. "You've
missed a bit."

"Where?"

Suresh kicked the ball against
the fence to make a big dirty
mark on the panels.

"There!"

He ran off, cackling, leaving
the furious Jagdish no choice
but to try and repair the
damage with his paintbrush.

"I'll get him back for that,"
he promised himself. "Just
wait. . ."

Jagdish had decided what he
was going to do by the time he
heard the bell. He hid the brush
behind the fence for later.

At the end of afternoon
school he ran all the way home
to make sure he got there first.
He still had another little
painting job to do before tea.

The howls of rage from his brother's bedroom could soon be heard all over the house. A wall poster of Suresh's favourite footballer now showed him more the colour of an American Indian!

The loud argument that
followed ended with a challenge
from Jagdish: "Bet my class can
beat yours any day."

" What — at football?" scoffed
Suresh.

"It's summer now," said
Jagdish. "Let's make it rounders."

"OK — fine by me. We'll
thrash you lot at anything."

Jagdish grinned. "Prove it!"

Chapter Three

Woof!

"Wicked!" cried Lee. "What a catch!"

"Good boy!" yelled Bradley.

The two friends had come back onto the school playing field after tea on Thursday to practise for the special challenge match.

They were not alone.

"Pity your dog can't play for us tomorrow," Lee said. "He's a star fielder. I hit that ball dead hard and he just gobbled it up."

"Yeah, trouble is, it takes ages to get the ball back off him," Bradley replied. "Come, Dylan. Here, boy!"

The little black mongrel ignored the command and frisked around with the tennis ball in his mouth. They chased after him until Dylan finally

grew tired of the game and lay down, drooling happily.

Lee grabbed the abandoned ball. "Ugh! It's all sticky now," he complained, wiping his hand on the grass. "That won't help my spinners."

Before Lee even had a chance
to bowl, however, they heard a
familiar rasping voice.

"Oi! You two – clear off! And
take that mutt with you as
well."

"Think Roll-On must mean you, Brad," Lee said cheekily.

"Watch it!" Bradley grinned. "C'mon, boy – home!"

"Woof!" responded Dylan, jumping to his feet. He wanted a drink.

The caretaker watched the trio trail away. "Little pests!" he muttered, scratching his stubbly chin. "Roll on the weekend – that's what I say."

Mr Smith still had a lot more painting to do before he could enjoy any break. He tried to get on with the job after school on Friday, despite all the noise coming from the playing field.

The rounders match had
already begun and class 4D
were struggling. Only Jagdish
had scored so far – and three
players were out!

Lee now took up position in the batting square. He swung wildly at the next ball from Suresh, missing it completely, and had to scamper to first base.

"C'mon, Brad!" Lee called out. "Show 'em how to do it."

Bradley, much to his own surprise, did actually manage to hit the ball.

"Run, stupid!" Jagdish
bellowed at him. "Don't just
stand there gawping at it. Run!"

Bradley jerked into
action and
set off, but
he had to
slam on
the brakes
to stop at
second
post as the
ball was returned ahead of him.

"That counts as half a
rounder," said Mrs Davison.
"Well done!"

They soon lost another batter to a run-out mix-up, but Shannon whacked the ball far enough away to jog around the track.

"We've still only got two and a half rounders," Jagdish told his team. "Reckon we're gonna need to double that at least."

They were helped on their way by high and wide no-balls.

"Another half-rounder," announced Mr Mackay, 5M's teacher, much to the disgust of Suresh.

"That's three," Jagdish grunted as he strode into the white square again, swishing his bat through the air for effect. "Now to make it four."

Suresh smirked at him. "Sorry, little brother, can't let you do that."

"Just belt up and bowl."

That's exactly what Suresh did. He made the ball spin and dip, deliberately keeping it low.

Jagdish was only able to scoop it away and he didn't even bother to run.

The fielder beyond second base took the catch and danced up and down in delight before being swamped by her team-mates.

"We're gonna win this dead easy," cried Suresh. "No sweat!"

To 4D's credit, they did make their opponents do some more running about in the warm sunshine. But only Lee and

Shannon — with her second
rounder — were able to add to the
total, giving a final score of five.

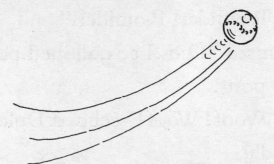

Lee had never struck the ball
so hard, smacking it way past
the small group of parents who
had come to watch the game.

Bradley's mum was
sunbathing instead, but it was a
good job that she had wrapped
Dylan's lead around her arm.

The dog tried to chase after the ball and nearly pulled her off the blanket.

"Rounder! Rounder!" chanted 4D as Lee galloped past the posts.

"Woof! Woof!" echoed Dylan loudly.

Chapter Four
Catch!

Suresh began 5M's reply in brilliant fashion. He gave Lee's first delivery such a thump that the ball was lost in the tall grass near the fence.

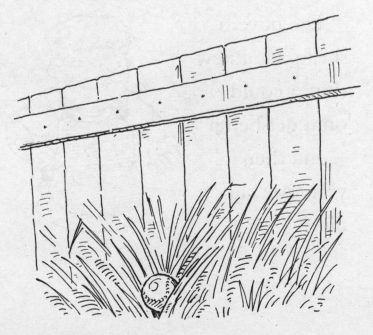

It took so long to find that the laughing Suresh could have completed his rounder on his hands and knees.

Jagdish was not best pleased. "You bowl any more rubbish like that and I'll take over," he called from his position at back-stop.

Lee gave a shrug. He knew things could only get better – and they very quickly did.

The next batter swished and
missed. She was also too slow to
set off and Jagdish's accurate
throw to Bradley at first post
ran her out.

That success helped to calm Lee's nerves and he settled into his usual bowling rhythm. By the time 5M managed to double their score, four players were already out.

Varying the angle of his run-up across the square, his arm speed and grip, Lee was making the ball swing and spin. He even surprised one batter with a donkey-drop delivery, which was only sliced away.

Bradley stepped
forward to make
the catch but
he took his eye
off the ball at
the last moment
and let it pop out
of his grasp.

"Butterfingers!" cried
Lee, adding to the chorus of
taunts from his
teammates.

"You couldn't
catch a cold!"
"You couldn't
catch a bus!"

"Never mind, Bradley," said Mrs Davison in sympathy. "But just remember the old saying – catches win matches!"

Suresh now came in for his second turn.

"On your toes, team," Jagdish ordered. "We want this guy out."

Suresh glanced round. "You lot won't get me out, Jag," he said with a smirk. "I'm gonna send this ball into orbit."

He was almost as good as his
word. The ball soared way into
the distance and no one really
fancied the long trek to fetch it.

Well, that's not quite true.
Somebody was already giving
chase.

"Dylan!" Bradley shouted.
"Come back!"

The dog had escaped his
mistress this time, yelping in
excitement. Dylan picked the
ball up in his mouth and

chewed at it while waiting to
see if anyone was going to join
in his game.

Mr Mackay approached the
dog warily. Dylan gave him a
sly grin and then ran off
towards the school, with the

teacher panting in pursuit.

Dylan raced round the corner of the building at full pelt and only narrowly avoided collision with a stepladder. The end of his trailing lead, however, became entangled with the bottom rung – and a lot of things seemed to happen all at once. . .

. . .Dylan was yanked to a
halt. . .

. . .the ball shot out of his
mouth. . .

. . .the ladder wobbled. . .

. . .a pot of paint flew up into
the air. . .

...and the caretaker clung
onto the drainpipe for dear
life...

"Aaaggghhh!"

Dylan broke free just as the
paint pot crashed to the floor,
sending its contents gushing

across the playground. He
turned back and paddled
through the spilt paint to sniff at
the red-coated ball. He didn't
like the smell of it any more and
trotted off as the teacher arrived
on the scene.

Mr Mackay
helped the
caretaker safely
down to the
ground. "Can't
leave you
hanging
around up
there," he smiled.

"Not when there's work to be done."

"What a mess!" grumbled Mr Smith, staring at the trail of red paw prints across the netball court. "Roll on my tea break – that's what I say."

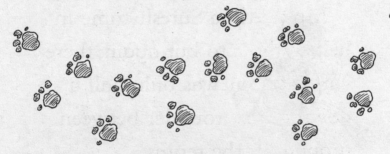

Mrs Davison produced a new ball to continue the game and Jagdish snatched it out of Lee's hand. "You go backstop instead,"

he ordered. "I'll show you how
to bowl."

Jagdish failed to
keep his promise.
Out of practice, he
bowled too many
no-balls and by the

time Suresh came in
to bat again, there
was only half a
rounder between
the teams.

In desperation, Jagdish copied
Lee's spinning action to try to
fool his brother, but Suresh
struck the ball high into the air.

Too high. As he set off around the track, Suresh realized he was in trouble. Out of the corner of his eye, he could see a fielder running to get underneath the ball. What Suresh didn't see was another figure scampering hotfoot – and red–pawed – towards it too.

"Mine!" called Bradley.

"Woof!" barked Dylan.

There was no way of avoiding the collision.

Making sure he kept his eyes firmly fixed on the ball this time, Bradley stretched out for it just as Dylan jumped up and sent him flying.

Bradley's right hand closed on the ball an instant before he hit the ground. His body lay spread-eagled across the grass, as if sunbathing, but he was holding the ball up in triumph.

"Wicked catch!" cried Lee,
helping the winded Bradley to
his feet.

"Thanks to Dylan," Bradley
grinned. "Don't reckon I'd have
reached it if he hadn't knocked
me over."

The dismissal of Suresh ended 5M's hopes of victory. 4D held onto their narrow lead better than anyone had been able to do with Dylan's. He was still running free.

"Wicked!" whooped Lee once more as the two brothers shook hands after the match. "What a win!"

"Woof!" agreed Dylan.

THE END

If you enjoyed this sporting tale, look out for another Sports Special by Rob Childs:

WICKED DAY!

And if you like football, you might like to read about the young footballers of Great Catesby Primary School in four smashing tales by Rob Childs, published by Corgi Pups Books:

GREAT GOAL!
GREAT HIT!
GREAT SAVE!
GREAT SHOT!